The Library of Higher Order Thinking Skills™

STRATEGIES FOR SYNTHESIS

PUTTING INFORMATION TOGETHER FOR CLASSROOM, HOMEWORK, AND TEST SUCCESS

JARED MEYER

The Library of Higher Order Thinking Skills™

Strategies for Synthesis

Putting Information Together
for Classroom, Homework,
and Test Success

Jared Meyer

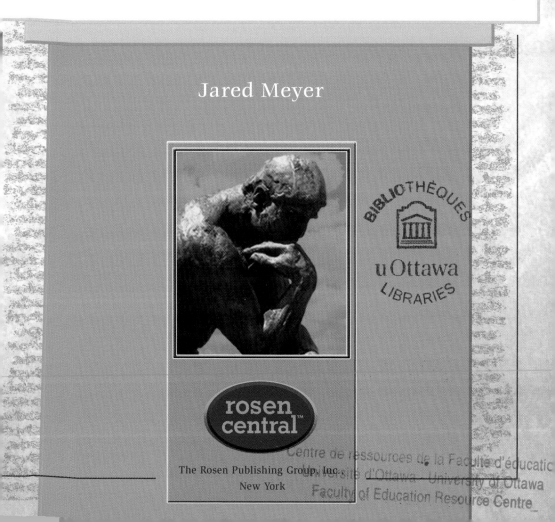

rosen
central™

The Rosen Publishing Group, Inc.
New York

b. 30155162

*To Dr. Michael Miller for introducing me to creativity from a brilliant
artist's perspective: his very own*

Published in 2006 by The Rosen Publishing Group, Inc.
29 East 21st Street, New York, NY 10010

371.3

First Edition

'M5987

2006

Library of Congress Cataloging-in-Publication Data

Meyer, Jared.
Strategies for synthesis : putting information together for classroom,
homework, and test success / Jared Meyer.—1st ed.
  p. cm. — (The library of higher order thinking skills)
Includes bibliographical references and index.
ISBN 1-4042-0475-X (lib. bdg.)
ISBN 1-4042-0658-2 (pbk. bdg.)
1. Study skills. 2. Critical thinking—Study and teaching
(Secondary). 3. Information retrieval—Study and teaching
(Secondary). 4. Academic achievement.
I. Title. II. Series.
LB1601.M49 2006
371.3'028'1—dc22

                                                    2004029319

Manufactured in the United States of America

On the cover: Portion of *The Thinker* by Auguste Rodin.

Cover (right corner inset), p. 1 © Royalty-Free/Nova Development
Corporation.

CONTENTS

Have you ever thought about how much information you come in contact with on a daily basis? There's the information provided in your schoolbooks, the information that your teachers share with you in class, and the information you receive from your local libraries, bookstores, and on the Internet. Then there's the information you receive from television, watching movies, and from conversations with your parents and friends. That's a lot of information and taking it all in can be a challenge.

Sometimes, you may be faced with way too much information and feel swamped. This is called quantitative overload. Other times, the depth of the information may be so over your head and difficult to understand that you may face qualitative overload. However, there is a solution to these problems. It's called synthesis, and it's a great skill to have.

Synthesis is the act of putting together useful information from different sources, determining which is the most important information, and using it appropriately in your schoolwork. The result could be a fresh, innovative answer to an exam question, a thoughtful essay, or an informative classroom presentation. In many ways, synthesis is like creativity. The more creativity that you use in your work, the easier it will be to accomplish your goals and be proud of the work that you've done.

This book will help you to succeed in school by guiding you to synthesize the information you receive. Whether you face an upcoming open-book test, a research paper, book report, or even a class presentation, knowing how to creatively put information together can help you get better grades—and make your entire school experience more enjoyable!

CHAPTER 1

Changing, Combining, Composing, and Constructing

There are a number of different strategies for synthesizing information. In this chapter, we will look at the strategies of changing, combining, composing, and constructing. Throughout, you'll find exercises that can help you practice these strategies. Give them a try. It's through practice that you'll master these skills.

Changing

When was the last time you were given a homework assignment or project where you had the choice of selecting a topic? Do you prefer having the freedom to decide what your work will be focused on, or do you prefer having fewer choices and being told exactly what to write about? One of the strategies for synthesis is the simple but sometimes significant act of changing information. If you were able to come up with the topic of an assignment, you could change your mind a dozen times until you discovered the perfect idea. Some students like having that choice when doing assignments.

Once you've decided the topic to investigate, you should begin by finding information from many sources. When you find the specific information that you want to use in your work, it's often necessary to change how the information is expressed while maintaining the original message. Doing this makes your work more personal and original. When using factual information from sources like books and encyclopedias, you may need to communicate those facts differently from how they are originally presented. This is known as paraphrasing. You may have to do this for a number of reasons. Information that you find applicable in an

Write It!

Take a look at an essay or lengthy written assignment that you already submitted and got back from your teacher. Looking at the first paragraph, how could you have **changed** it while still communicating the very same message? On a separate sheet of paper, rewrite the paragraph so that it says the same thing as before, but uses at least ten words fewer.

encyclopedia, for example, may be too lengthy or complicated for the assignment that you're working on, so changing the information to fit the style of your work may be helpful. Also, repeating the information without crediting the source would be an act of plagiarism, which is never a good idea.

You can put together an original product of work by selecting the key elements from the source, changing how they are presented, and maintaining their accuracy. For example, imagine you are asked to write a short research paper on the weapons and artillery that were used in the U.S. Civil War. Using a reference book, you may come to a lengthy section on the Ironclad, a type of warship. Given that you would want your research paper to be written with your own original style, you could refer to just a few main points from the book. Taking a few snippets of information will allow you to elaborate on those facts and change the ideas found in the book into your own ideas.

Combining

Do you know what makes a peanut butter and jelly sandwich so appetizing? It's the combination of the three ingredients that makes it a delicious lunchtime sandwich. If you've ever made such a sandwich yourself, you know that it isn't very difficult to do. Believe it or not, making a sandwich is related to your class work.

Did You Know?

People often **combine** their talents in order to get a project done. For example:

- A writer and an artist **combine** their talents to create an illustrated book.

- A painter, carpenter, mason, plumber, and electrician **combine** their skills to make a house.

- A recording engineer and a musician **combine** their talents to create a record.

Combining, another strategy for synthesis, can be used to create a unique and original product. For example, if you are doing a book report you might use information provided by multiple sources and combine them into one outstanding, thoughtful statement or paragraph.

Not only can you combine information from different sources, but you can also combine two or more statements from the same source. Take a book on sea creatures, for example. It may provide information on whales and mention that they are among the largest creatures on the planet. It may also state that they are mammals, that they rarely attack humans, and that they have a lifespan of up to ninety years. If you don't think that it is necessary

to mention all of these points, you could easily high-
light two or three of them, and combine them into a
sentence or paragraph. For example, you might use
a few of the previous facts to write:

*Whales may be large, but they are not a threat
to humans.*

As you can see, two facts about whales (that
they are large and that they rarely attack humans)
were combined to create an original sentence.

Composing

Compose means to put together or to create. Often,
the word is used in the music world. People who
write music are known as composers. But it also
applies to other situations. In an academic setting,
you may be called upon by your teachers to compose
an original essay or story.

Imagine that you are asked to compose an
essay about your favorite color. In this essay, you
could provide your own thoughts, and you could
also include information from outside sources. For
example, you might write about the color blue and
explain in detail why you like it. You might
describe how the color makes you feel, and you
might provide a list of all the blue things you own.
In addition, you might include a statement or two
about the color blue from a well-known poet or

Try It!
....

See if you can do the following:

• **Compose** a four-line poem that rhymes using the names of two people you've recently learned about in school.

• **Compose** a short story in which you and your best friend switch places for a day.

• **Compose** a list of ten things you would need if you were stranded on a desert island.

jazz musician. This will give an outside perspective on the topic and may make the composition more interesting to other people.

Constructing

Have you ever constructed a small colorful house using LEGOs or some other type of building blocks? The last time you went to the beach, did you attempt to construct a sand castle? In art class do you enjoy being creative and constructing art from a variety of materials? If you do, then you're not alone. Some students find their art classes more interesting than their math classes because of the creativity that is required.

The very same strategy of constructing things in art class is often used in other classes, especially when it comes to classroom presentations and group projects. For example, your social studies teacher may ask you to construct a model of a medieval castle. Your teacher may also request additional research to make the project more educational for you and your classmates. Perhaps you have to give a class presentation describing the major characteristics of the castle. Or maybe you are assigned to write a short essay that describes the type of people who would have lived in your castle. In fact, the research you do could be just as important as the building of the castle itself. That's an important point to remember: when constructing anything, make sure you've done enough research to properly complete the task.

Creating, Designing, Finding an Unusual Way, and Formulating

In this chapter, we will continue to look at strategies used for synthesizing information. As before, there will be short practice exercises that are designed to be both fun and educational.

Creating

Are you familiar with the story of Frankenstein? In this story, a mad scientist creates a living person from a variety of dead materials. It may seem strange, but this is an example of how we can go about creating things at school. Like the mad scientist Dr. Frankenstein, we can start with an idea and use materials that are available to us to create something bigger. In our case, however, this would be an essay or an art project instead of a monster.

Some assignments that you may be given at school could be as simple as creating a chart showing your height and weight over the years since you

Did You Know?

Many different occupations allow people to express their **creativity**. Some of the most well-known of these occupations involve painting, photography, writing, architecture, and fashion design. However, there are many other jobs out there that appeal to people with **creative** minds. Some of these are:

- A chef chooses among many available ingredients to **create** tasty and visually appealing meals.

- A Web designer **creates** Web sites that look good, are easy to use, and attract visitors.

- A scientist uses his or her **creativity** to design original experiments.

- A teacher **creates** lesson plans in order to engage his or her class.

- A retail manager has to use his or her **creativity** to choose the best ways to display products for sale.

were born. Another assignment might be to create a graph depicting an average child's growth span over his or her first ten years, using information that your teacher provides you. When it comes to creating something new such as a graph or picture, there may be endless possibilities of how your end product will look. Following directions and adding your personal creative style will help you to do your best on your assignments.

Designing

Can you recall the basic design of the Empire State Building in New York City? How about the basic structure of the Washington Monument in our nation's capital? Before there was a celebratory groundbreaking ceremony or even before the first brick was laid, the people behind these buildings used the strategy of designing to plan the glorious structures. Designing is the strategy that is often accomplished during the beginning stages of a project.

When preparing to answer a lengthy exam question, you may design how to go about answering the question given the information that you have. For example, if you had an exam in health class on the topic of nutrition, you might see a question about how to design a well-balanced breakfast. As an answer, you could detail a nutritious meal that you and your friends would prefer.

Write It!

Design a perfect solitary Saturday afternoon. Write it out on a separate piece of paper. Now take that idea and design a new plan, but this time including your friends. Finally, take that new idea and design a third plan, this time including your family, too. Did your first design differ greatly from your second design? Did your third design differ greatly from your second design?

Designing this meal would require using the information you have learned, such as which foods are good for you, as well as mentioning the types of nutritious food that you and your friends personally like. Answering in such a manner is not only informative and correct, but also interesting because it is personal and original.

Finding an Unusual Way

Have you ever heard the expression "thinking outside of the box"? As you may know, it means thinking in a nontraditional manner or in an unusual way. Of course, by unusual we don't mean "strange" or "weird" but instead something that is original.

As you have noticed throughout this book, creativity can play an important role in applying certain strategies to your schoolwork. The strategy of finding an unusual way is, in itself, unusual compared to the other strategies, as it requires a good deal of extraordinary creativity to implement it successfully.

When it comes to classroom exams, an excellent strategy is to find an unusual way to answer the questions. In addition to providing accurate information, imagine how much you'd stand out

Answer It!

Consider the following three ways to give a classroom presentation on the early history of the United States of America:

A) Dressing up as Abraham Lincoln and re-creating a scene from his reading of the Gettysburg Address.

B) Handing out a copy of the Bill of Rights to each student in the audience and then reading selections from the document.

C) Reading a speech on the ratification of the Constitution from a number of note cards.

Which one of the ways do you think would be most interesting to the audience? Which one of the ways do you think would be most fun to present?

from your classmates if you looked at a question from a different angle. If you're facing a question that is completely stumping you, perhaps you can find an unusual way to answer the question.

Finding an unusual way to do group projects, to write essays or research papers, or to give classroom presentations will help convince your teacher that you are quite the creative student. At the same time, it will also probably make the assignments more fun for you.

Formulating

Formulating, one of the twenty-two strategies covered in this book, is another word for devising or developing. For assignments like essays, you've probably learned that a formula for writing them consists of having a beginning, a middle, and an end. You've also probably come across formulas in math class. In each case, a formula is something that is consistently followed. In many ways, it's like a rule. So when we formulate something, we are looking to create a rule for how something should be done.

Imagine that you are about to begin working on a homework assignment that requires you to use your textbooks and classroom notes. If your teacher has given you ten questions to answer, it would be a good idea to answer each question thoroughly by formulating the answers using your resources. This means you would use the same process each time. You would also want to keep your writing style consistent, and each time answer the questions based on what you know the teacher is looking for.

While formulating, you could ask yourself questions like: Should I formulate a series of important events in my explanation? Is there a certain question-answering formula that the teacher is looking for? Should I just use the information from my class notes? Do I include my opinion in my answers? Should I just state the facts? By answering these questions, you will develop a formula to guide you.

As you can see, formulas are not just for scientists and mathematicians, but also for students like you to use when putting together information. They are the tools you use to consistently develop an argument, whether it is in math class, history class, or English class.

CHAPTER

3

Generating, Inventing, Planning, and Originating

Let's move on and look at a few more strategies for synthesis. Like before, these are strategies that will test your creativity. As you are going through this chapter, think about ways you can apply these strategies in your own life. Don't just think about school; think also about how these strategies can apply outside of school.

Generating

Have you ever taken out a blank sheet of notebook paper and generated ideas about different fun things you would like to do? If you haven't, you should try it sometime. A local newspaper could act as a guide for upcoming events in your hometown and the surrounding area. Or simply use your imagination—what are a few things you've always wanted to do but haven't got around to doing yet?

Believe it or not, the same strategy used to generate ideas may be helpful in completing your school assignments. For example, have you ever been asked to generate a list of reasons why a historical event occurred? Or maybe you've been asked to come

Write It!

On a separate sheet of paper, **generate** a list of five basic reasons why school is important to your development as a person.

up with a number of items that support a specific theory. These are just a couple of ways that the strategy of generating can be useful. Of course, there are many more.

Inventing

Have you ever come up with a really impressive idea that may not be so well known? What do you think are the world's three best inventions? You may be called upon to do an assignment in school that requires complete originality and 100 percent creativity on your part. The strategy of inventing new ideas is easy to explain, but often difficult to do. That's because it takes a sharp mind and lots of effort from the inventor.

Imagine you are studying the life of Alexander Graham Bell, the inventor of the telephone. Your teacher gives the class an assignment to invent a new product that could help your classmates. In preparing to come up with a few good ideas, you might study some inventions that have already been created. Then, using your creativity and even "thinking outside of the box," you might brainstorm a list of products that you would like to create. Then, you would have to think about what it would take to create that product. Would you have the time, money, and materials? After considering all these factors, you would be ready to choose the best project for the assignment.

Try It!

Invent a new way to answer questions. In what new ways could students express their answers other than writing them down on paper? (For example, students might videotape their answers.)

Planning

Does it seem as though your teachers always have a plan for each and every class? Can you imagine how much time would be wasted if they didn't have their strategies of teaching worked out ahead of time? Good planning is just as important for working on assignments as it is for being a good teacher. If you are given a group project to work on with your classmates, you will all plan the best way to divide responsibilities and present specific information. If you have a paper to write on your own, you will be sure to plan how many hours you will need to complete the assignment and do the best job possible.

Planning is a first step in putting information together. Without it, your final product may be of low quality and may not be completed in a timely

Did You Know?

When **planning** an essay, keep the following tips in mind:

• Create a timetable. Estimate how much time you will need to do your research, to write the first draft, and to revise the first draft. Make sure you stick to your schedule.

• Don't be afraid to ask your teacher for advice. If you get stuck, your teacher can always offer you tips on the best way to get the assignment done.

• Create an outline. After the research has been completed, the outline is used to plan the actual writing. Your outline should break down your essay paragraph by paragraph, indicating what the main points will be.

fashion. There's no doubt about it—good grades always start with a good plan.

Originating

Have you ever felt frustrated when you just couldn't seem to come up with a new idea? Believe it or not, some of the best ideas that have been created were based on concepts or theories that already existed. You may find that the best way or even the only way to respond to questions on exams or homework assignments is by origi-nating—developing something new while using supportive information to back up your answers.

Originating is similar to inventing because the quality of what is created is unique in one way or another and comes from an original source. Sometimes new ideas may originate from the research you do, so be sure to take good notes while doing your research. Your notes show your teachers that not only are you fulfilling the research portion of the assignment, but that you're taking an active role in the learning process.

Predicting, Pretending, and Producing

In this chapter we'll cover three more strategies for synthesis: predicting, pretending, and producing. These three strategies all require you to use your imagination and are among the most fun strategies to practice. We hope you'll agree!

Predicting

Do you know what the weather forecast is for tomorrow? Did you know that predicting next week's weather is based on a variety of sources of information? Like meteorologists can predict weather, you, too, have the resources and knowledge to predict what your teacher is looking for on an assignment or test question. You can also use the strategy of predicting while working on assignments to help you do them accurately.

If you've had your teacher for a good period of time, you can probably

Try It!
....

Predict what would happen in the following hypothetical situations. How would you be affected?

• You get straight As this year.
• Your best friend fails math class this year.
• Your family hosts an exchange student from France.
• Your school decides to eliminate all after-school sports.

predict what it is that he or she is looking for in your answers. Beyond the right information, your teacher probably wants to see proper grammar and clear penmanship. While you're designing a classroom presentation, you can predict your classmates' responses. Will they think you've found an interesting and unusual way to present the information? By predicting the results of your actions, you'll be able to provide exactly what your teacher or audience is looking for.

Predicting can be a rewarding strategy for putting information together. Looking at new information in different ways and trying one method of synthesis over another, you may predict how your work will be evaluated. This will give you a few more tools to help you complete your assignments. Predicting will help you give outstanding and original class presentations, write inspirational research papers and essays, and answer test questions that demand more than just the facts.

Figure It Out

Here's a mathematical example: Can you **predict** what the next two numbers will be in this series: 2, 4, 6, 8 . . . ? What about this one: 1, 3, 9, 27 . . . ?

For the first example, the answer is 10, 12 (each number is the sum of 2 and the previous number). For the second example, the answer is 81, 243 (each number in the sequence is multiplied by 3 to generate the next number).

Pretending

For fun, how often do you pretend to be someone you are not? Pretending is often easy to do alone or with friends, but for some students, it is difficult to pretend in front of your classmates and teachers. You may remember playing games with your friends, pretending that you were explorers, seeking out new creatures in the wild, or pretending that you were masked crime fighters on the lookout for dangerous villains. These experiences may actually help you in your studies. When appropriate, including in your class work or take-home assignments, pretending can often make your

Write It!

Think about the main characters from the last two books that you read. **Pretend** that they all meet each other to talk about their main struggles in each of their stories. Will they have any feelings in common? Will they be able to relate to each other? Write out your answer in a few short paragraphs on a separate sheet of paper.

work more fun and satisfying.

Pretending can be an enjoyable and effective strategy in using information from different places. You can imagine being the main character of a book you are reading and pretend that his or her experiences are your experiences, too. If you are writing a book report and your teacher requests a description of the character's feelings during a significant event in the book, you can access similar emotions by pretending you are that character. Pretending allows you to see the world through another person's eyes and helps you understand his or her actions.

Producing

Have you ever been involved in a school play or musical? If you have, then you know how much work goes into such a production. Producing is also a strategy that is often used to do schoolwork, especially when using an array of materials or information. Each project a student works on is a production, whether he or she does it alone or with classmates. If you and a few of your classmates are asked to put together a presentation using poster boards, you and your team members would be responsible for producing or manufacturing that extensive project. The entire team would be responsible for every detail of the project from start to finish. Based on the requirements of the assignment, you and your team members may have a lot of flexibility in what the final project will communicate and what it will ultimately look like.

The strategy of producing such a group project may include many of the strategies already covered in this book. Producing a group project, especially when you have very little to start with, can be a challenge. But if the team works together and everyone does their part, the experience of production can be immensely satisfying.

CHAPTER 5

Rearranging, Reorganizing, Revising, and Reconstructing

This chapter deals with improving your work by making changes to your initial ideas. The four strategies we will cover are rearranging, reorganizing, revising, and reconstructing. Like the other strategies, these ones are about being creative and thinking outside of the box. They are especially helpful when you are working on the second draft of a paper, or if you want to add spice to a piece of writing that didn't exactly come out like you had hoped.

Rearranging

Baseball and softball coaches often rearrange their lineups. For example, a coach might replace a slow outfielder with a faster one, or switch a left-handed hitter with a right-handed one. The purpose of these changes is to give the team a better chance of winning the game. Similarly, when a teacher returns an assignment to you requesting corrections, all you may need to do to improve your work is tweak some of your statements. Often, the best strategy to go about doing this is rearranging.

Rearranging is defined as switching around the order of content. It can be used to make content original and better stated. Sometimes, the order of two or three sentences could be rearranged to make a clearer point. Other times, perhaps an entire paragraph could be moved elsewhere in the document or even removed completely to obtain optimum results. Rearranging

Answer It!

Choose the best way to **rearrange** the following sentence:

Because it had a headache, the brown cow decided not to jump over the river and instead returned to the barn.

A) The brown cow decided not to jump over the river because it had a headache. Instead, it returned to the barn.

B) Because it had a headache, the brown cow returned to the barn. Instead, it decided not to jump over the river.

Sentence A is the best choice. It keeps the meaning of the original sentence better than sentence B.

is often done on homework assignments when you want to make statements easier to understand or to communicate a general comment in a different manner.

Be careful, though, as rearranging information may lead to changing the entire context of a statement. Rearranging, like other strategies, should be done when it is appropriate and not just to make your final work slightly different.

Reorganizing

While organizing a paper or project, have you noticed that your first few ideas are sometimes the worst you'll come up with? Has changing a few ideas and reorganizing those original thoughts ever inspired you? Reorganizing is a strategy that is often used in synthesizing information from a variety of resources. It's a great strategy because it allows you to experiment.

Let's imagine for a moment that you are working on a book report. You may have one idea on how to approach the topic before you have even begun your research. Upon researching your topic and determining what information you want to use, you may change your mind, come up with an even better idea, and perhaps reorganize your outline. This may mean that you choose to switch the order of the details that you will cover or simply reorganize the flow of your essay. Similar to reconstructing, reorganizing is done to satisfy the needs of the person judging your work, to improve its quality, and make you feel confident that your product is exceptional.

Try It!

Here is a practice example related to **reorganizing**.

What would happen if you were to **reorganize** the contents in your school locker or closet at home? Would it improve their current conditions or worsen them?

Revising

Isn't it a great feeling to receive an assignment back from a teacher with little or even no corrections noted in the margins? Have you ever received a paper back from a teacher with so many comments that you are asked to revise and resubmit it? Revising is the strategy of reading over something and correcting for errors in spelling, grammar, content, and how the document flows when it is read. This strategy also allows you to make final changes to your work in order to improve its quality. Ideally, the more you revise your work before submitting it, the better it will turn out and you'll increase your chances of getting a good grade.

Write It!

Revise the following paragraph on a separate sheet of paper. Make sure to correct all errors in spelling and grammar. Also, try to make your **revision** easier to read than the original.

Basketball is a sport maid up of six players on a team. When they play together its important to show teamwork. This makes the game fun and everyone has a best chance of winning. Basketball is the type of game where the beat team wins and not the best individual players. It's also a game that takes a lot of effort.

Revising can be easy if it is done with good intentions. By actively seeking out errors in your own work prior to handing it in, you will prove to your teacher that you have thoughtfully completed the assignment and cared about its quality.

Reconstructing

Have you ever put a lot of work into an assignment only to find out that your teacher was looking for something totally different? It's happened to everyone at some time, but it doesn't always have to be entirely bad news. The good news could be that you are asked to reconstruct, or rebuild, part of the project rather than start all over again. Reconstructing gives you the chance to improve upon something if it doesn't come out as planned or if it doesn't meet the requirements of the assignment.

You have probably reconstructed numerous projects and essays in the past even before submitting them to your teachers. Sometimes you may have constructed them more than once. While having to reconstruct work you've already completed may seem disappointing and frustrating, the activity is actually excellent practice in preparing you for the development of future projects. Whether your initial outline needs to be totally reconstructed or just a few minor details altered, constructing and reconstructing often go hand in hand during the creative process.

Chapter 6

Supposing, Visualizing, and Writing

Only three more strategies remain in our study of synthesis. This chapter introduces you to those three important strategies: supposing, visualizing, and writing. Like before, there are suggestions for practice exercises to help develop your skills.

Supposing

Have you ever imagined what it would be like if you moved to another country? Suppose only you were to move and your family remained back home. Such questions are certainly thrilling and possibly even a little scary to think about. Questions, like these, however, can often lead to fresh ideas and exciting outcomes in your schoolwork.

While writing an essay in class, you may want to throw in a dash of mystery and intrigue by challenging your readers with statements that use the word "suppose." For example, while writing a paper on Abraham Lincoln you may want to pose a thought-provoking question such as, "Suppose Lincoln lived to 85 years of age. Would our country be any different today?" Depending on your teacher and his or her writing requirements, including such a statement is a good way to add spice to your writing and make it more interesting. Asking "suppose" questions while doing your research can also be helpful, in addition to making research more fun.

Write It!

Suppose people are no longer permitted to fly on airplanes and that only the flight crew and cargo are allowed. How would this affect people who vacation in distant places and people who do business all over the country? What alternative methods of transportation would be available? Write your answer in a few short paragraphs on a separate sheet of paper.

Visualizing

A wonderful strategy to use while doing schoolwork is visualizing. Before even starting to organize your thoughts or plan of action, try closing your eyes for a few minutes and imagining pictures that relate to the work that you are about to do. If you have an oral presentation to give, visualize standing in front of your classmates. Imagine that they are all smiling supportively, hoping that you'll do well. By taking a moment to visualize success, you'll increase your chances of doing a great job.

While you are beginning to plan your project, you may try to visualize the resources you will need and the connections they will make to your final product. Although visualizing may not necessarily motivate you to write down ideas, with the

Try It!

Try the following:

- **Visualize** a strategy to get home from school as quickly as possible.
- **Visualize** where you would like to go on vacation this year.
- **Visualize** what you would buy if you won a $500 gift certificate to your favorite store.
- **Visualize** what you would say if you were able to have dinner with your favorite actor.

right attitude it will affect the quality of your work and the pleasure you derive from doing it.

Writing

If you had to do an assignment, would you prefer a classroom presentation or a book report? Of these two forms of communication, writing is sometimes preferred over speaking because it can be saved, read, and judged at another time. As you have already experienced, a good portion of your work both inside and outside of the classroom is based on your ability to communicate by writing. Many assignments require writing, and even those that are presentation-based may also require written documentation to support them. When putting together a paper or presentation, it is always a good idea to jot down personal notes and make mental connections along the way.

The schoolwork that you do on a daily basis in class and the projects you put together at home will consistently require good writing skills. Most of the skills covered in this book can often be implemented by writing.

Write It!

On a separate sheet of paper, **write** a paragraph describing yourself. Was it easy to express yourself this way? Do you think speaking about yourself would have been easier?

Wrap-up

This book has covered twenty-two helpful strategies for synthesis. That is a good deal of information that can be used to prepare for exams, to do research, and to put information together for projects, papers, and presentations.

While there may be many strategies covered in this book, the more you use them, the more organized and prepared you will be to complete your assignments and do a great job. Before you know it, you may find yourself naturally using these strategies in much of what you do inside and outside of the classroom.

GLOSSARY

applicable Relevant and appropriate.

array A collection, selection, or arrangement.

brainstorm To spontaneously think, suggest, or come up with many ideas.

context What surrounds a word or passage; often it can be used to shed light on what the word or passage means.

depict To describe or illustrate.

devise To come up with a way of doing something.

hypothetical Something that hasn't happened, but is meant to be imagined.

implement To apply or put into action.

meteorologist Someone who studies weather, such as a weatherman.

optimum Best, finest, or most favorable.

plagiarism To copy someone else's writing and claim it is your own.

qualitative Relating to or based on quality.

quantitative Relating to or based on quantity.

tweak To make small adjustments.

unison Agreement or harmony.

WEB SITES

Due to the changing nature of Internet links, the Rosen Publishing Group, Inc., has developed an online list of Web sites related to the subject of this book. This site is updated regularly. Please use this link to access the list:

http://www.rosenlinks.com/lhots/stsy

FOR FURTHER READING

Ernst, John. *Middle School Study Skills*. Westminster, CA: Teacher Created Resources, 1996.

Fisher, Alec. *Critical Thinking: An Introduction*. New York, NY: Cambridge University Press, 2001.

Forte, Imogene, and Sandra Schurr. *180 Icebreakers to Strengthen Critical Thinking and Problem-Solving Skills*. Nashville, TN: Incentive Publications, 1999.

Gilbert, Sara. *How to Do Your Best on Tests*. New York, NY: William Morrow & Company, 1998.

James, Elizabeth, and Carol Barkin. *How to Be School Smart*. New York, NY: William Morrow & Company, 1998.

BIBLIOGRAPHY

Barber, Peggy. "Higher Order Thinking Skills." Memphis City Schools. Retrieved September 2004 (http://www. memphis-schools.k12.tn.us/schools/ magnolia.es/highorder.htm).

Guy, Bob. "Using the Internet to Teach Higher Order Thinking Skills in U.S. History Classes." Metropolitan Nashville Public Schools. Retrieved September 2004 (http://www.nashville-schools. davidson.k12.tn.us/CurriculumAwards/ Higher_Order_Thinking.html).

Hammond, Glen. "Instruction That Works— Higher Order Thinking Skills." Retrieved September 2004 (http://xnet. rrc.mb.ca/glenh/hots.htm).

Jensen, Eric. "How Julie's Brain Learns." Camels Hump Middle School. December 16, 1999. Retrieved September 2004 (http://www.chms.k12.vt.us/ article2.htm).

Petty, Pam. "Higher Order Thinking Skills." Pam Petty's Educational Resources. August 21, 2003. Retrieved September 2004 (http://www.pampetty.com/ hots.htm).

Pogrow, Stanley. "Research Based and Scientifically Validated." HOTS. Retrieved September 2004 (http://www.hots.org/research.html).

Southeastern Louisiana University. "What is Higher Order Thinking?" Retrieved September 2004 (http://www.selu.edu/Academics/Education/TEC/think.htm).

University of Maryland University College. "Using Bloom's Taxonomy in Assignment Design." Retrieved September 2004 (http://www.umuc.edu/prog/ugp/ewp/bloomtax.html).

INDEX

About the Author

Jared Meyer is an author and educator who works with students on improving their decision-making and communication skills. As a program facilitator, he has lectured at the University of California, San Diego and the University of Maryland, College Park. In addition to writing *Strategies for Recalling Knowledge* and *Strategies for Synthesis*, he has published thirteen articles on student development.

Designer: Nelson Sá; Editor: Brian Belval